For Amelie Giulia, my first grandchild

Library of Congress catalog card number: 96-62032
Published simultaneously in Canada by HarperCollins*CanadaLtd*
Printed and bound in Italy
First published in Great Britain by Andersen Press, 1997
First American edition, 1997

Prince Peter and the Teddy Bear

David McKee

Farrar, Straus and Giroux New York

"It's your birthday in seven days, Prince Peter," said the King. "I expect you'd like a silver sword."

“No, sir. Please, sir, I’d like a teddy bear,” said Prince Peter.
“A TEDDY BEAR?” said the King. “HUMPH!”

“It’s your birthday in six days, Prince Peter,” said the Queen the next day. “I’m sure you want a new crown.”

“Please, ma’am, I’d like a teddy bear,” said Prince Peter.
“A TEDDY BEAR?” said the Queen. “HUH!”

“It’s your birthday in five days, Prince Peter,” said the King.
“I bet you’d like a big white horse.”

"Please, sir, I'd like a teddy bear," said Prince Peter.
"GRRRRR!" said the King.

"It's your birthday in four days, Prince Peter," said the Queen. "I know you'd like a throne for your room."

“Please, ma’am, I’d like a teddy bear,” said Prince Peter.
“AAAAAH!” said the Queen.

"Only three days to your birthday, Prince Peter,"
said the King. "You can have a suit of armor."

"Please, sir, I'd like a teddy bear," said Prince Peter.
"YEUIEEEE!" moaned the King.

"Two days to your birthday, Prince Peter," said the Queen.
"How about a nice new coach for processions?"

“Please, ma’am, I’d like a teddy bear,” said Prince Peter.
“OOOOOOH!” sighed the Queen.

"It's Prince Peter's birthday tomorrow," said the King.
"What can we give him?"
"Oh, for goodness' sake, give him a teddy bear,"
said the Queen.

“Happy birthday, Prince Peter,” said the King and Queen, and they gave him a very heavy present.
“Thank you, sir. Thank you, ma’am,” said Prince Peter.

"It's a teddy bear," said the Queen.
"A golden teddy bear," said the King.
"Thank you, sir. Thank you, ma'am," said Prince Peter.

"Good night, sir. Good night, ma'am," said Prince Peter at bedtime. He took his present with him.

“Solid gold,” he sighed. “How awful.” And he put Teddy on the chest of drawers.
He was awakened by sobbing. Teddy was crying. “What’s wrong?” asked Prince Peter.

"I want to be cuddled," sniffed Teddy.
"But you're hard and cold!" said Prince Peter.
"I know," sobbed Teddy. "But I still want a cuddle.
Everyone needs a cuddle."

“Come on, then,” said Prince Peter, and he cuddled Teddy. Very uncomfortable, he thought. But after a while he murmured, “Strange, he’s really rather cuddly.” With that, he fell asleep.

In the morning, Teddy was cuddlier than ever.
"You aren't hard and cold at all now,"
said Prince Peter, smiling.
"That's because you cuddled me," said Teddy.

“Morning, Dad!” said Prince Peter when he went to breakfast. Then he gave the King a cuddle.
“Oh, ah! Morning, Peter,” said the King, smiling.

"Good morning, Mom!" said Prince Peter, and he gave her a cuddle, too.
"Good morning, Peter," said the Queen, smiling.
"How's Teddy?"

“Wonderful, thanks,” said Prince Peter.
“I wonder what you’ll want for Christmas?” said the King.

"Come on, Dad," said Prince Peter with a smile. "Eat your cornflakes before they go soggy."